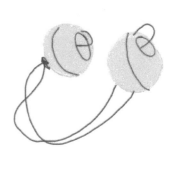

Daydreamers Press
www.daydreamerspress.com
Manufactured in the United States of America
ISBN 978-0-9996613-1-4

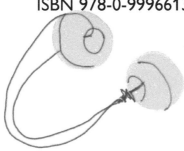

In loving memory of my father, Gary Penn Sr. (1957-2011), who first dreamed up The Turtle With An Afro, and asked me to write the book when I was young and had no plans to create children's literature. You knew I would one day bring her to life.
Thank you for this dream, and for your love.

To my mother, who first read to me, who taught me and
so many others to love reading, and who encouraged me to write.

For my treasures, Jember and Zemen, always…
- Carlotta Penn

To Niyi, Ife, and Sarai, my best critiques.
- Audy Popoola

Be Dynamite!
CMSP 2022

The TURTLE with an AFRO

Turtle was frustrated.
It was a *bad hair day*...

Her springy, sprightly curls
absolutely, positively
would not stay in place!

They refused to obey the

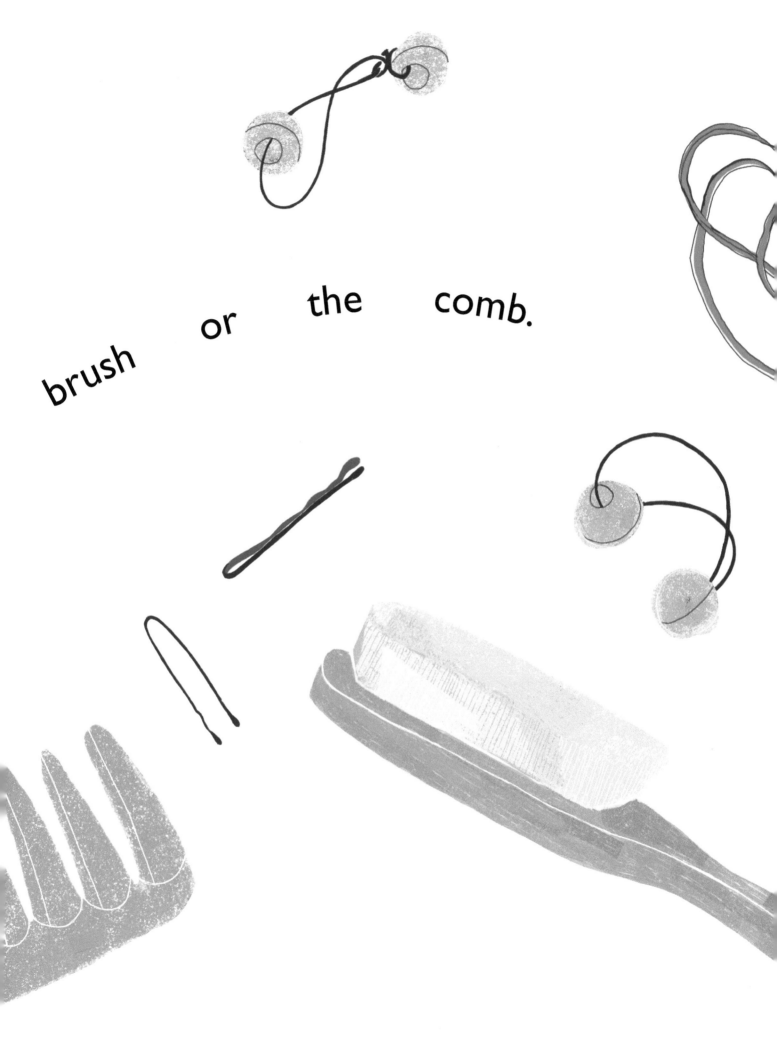

brush or the comb.

They did not care how
loud she screamed...

...or how long she moaned.

They were fantastic, fabulous, frolicking, and fiesty!

"Why oh why," Turtle asked,

"won't you just be nice to me?"

But those crazy curls had extravagant plans to dance, and jump, and bounce all over her head.

Shimmy, shimmy, shimmy, slip, slide, twirl!

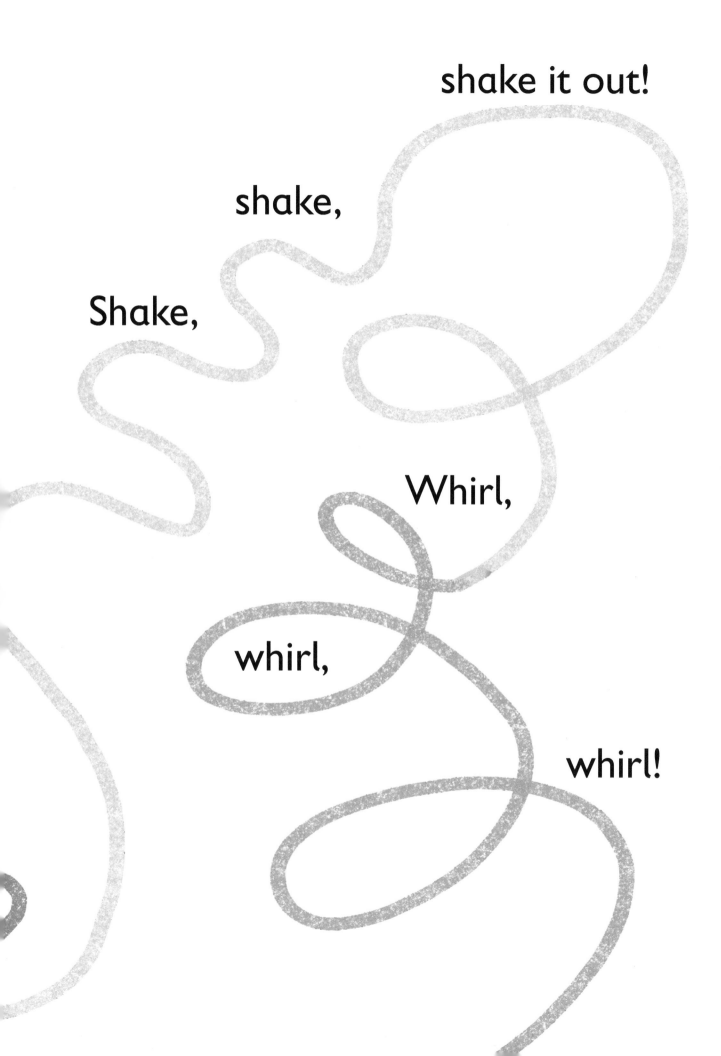

shake it out!

shake,

Shake,

Whirl,

whirl,

whirl!

Turtle watched them
twist and turn,
full of shimmer
and shine.

"A thousand works of art,"
she thought,

"and each one
is mine!"

She whipped her head
around and around.
Jumped back, forth,
up and down.

Stylin' and profilin'
with her lovely locs...

Turtle was ready to rock!

So just like that turtle saw the light.
Her curls were absolutely, positively...

D NA
Y

MITE!

"Flow fierce and fly free!" Turtle said.
And look at that Afro...

A crown on her head!

Dr. Carlotta Penn lives with her husband and two children, Jember Dove and Zemen Phoenix, in Columbus, OH.

Gary M. Penn, Sr., pictured left.

Pictured to the right is Aubrey Taylor, the late father of Audy Popoola. He was an amazing individual whose character continues to influence her to this day. Audy Popoola currently lives in Upper Marlboro, MD with her loving husband and beautiful children.